Dear Parents:

Congratulations! Your child is ta...
the first steps on an exciting jour...
The destination? Independent reading!

STEP INTO READING® will help your child get there. The program offers five steps to reading success. Each step includes fun stories and colorful art or photographs. In addition to original fiction and books with favorite characters, there are Step into Reading Non-Fiction Readers, Phonics Readers and Boxed Sets, Sticker Readers, and Comic Readers—a complete literacy program with something to interest every child.

Learning to Read, Step by Step!

Ready to Read   Preschool–Kindergarten
• big type and easy words • rhyme and rhythm • picture clues
For children who know the alphabet and are eager to begin reading.

Reading with Help   Preschool–Grade 1
• basic vocabulary • short sentences • simple stories
For children who recognize familiar words and sound out new words with help.

Reading on Your Own   Grades 1–3
• engaging characters • easy-to-follow plots • popular topics
For children who are ready to read on their own.

Reading Paragraphs   Grades 2–3
• challenging vocabulary • short paragraphs • exciting stories
For newly independent readers who read simple sentences with confidence.

Ready for Chapters   Grades 2–4
• chapters • longer paragraphs • full-color art
For children who want to take the plunge into chapter books but still like colorful pictures.

STEP INTO READING® is designed to give every child a successful reading experience. The grade levels are only guides; children will progress through the steps at their own speed, developing confidence in their reading.

Remember, a lifetime love of reading starts with a single step!

www.barbie.com

Published in the United States by Random House Children's Books, a division of Penguin Random House LLC, 1745 Broadway, New York, NY 10019, and in Canada by Penguin Random House Canada Limited, Toronto.

Step into Reading, Random House, and the Random House colophon are registered trademarks of Penguin Random House LLC.

Visit us on the Web!
rhcbooks.com

Educators and librarians, for a variety of teaching tools, visit us at RHTeachersLibrarians.com

ISBN 978-0-593-80739-2 (trade) — ISBN 978-0-593-80740-8 (lib. bdg.)

Printed in the United States of America

10 9 8 7 6 5 4 3 2 1

Barbie™

YOU CAN BE A HORSE RIDER

adapted by Bria Lymon

based on a story by Gina Gold

illustrated by Mattel and Susanna Amatti

Random House 🏠 New York

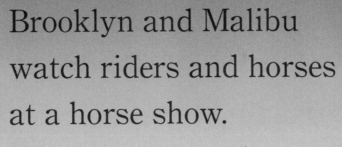

Brooklyn and Malibu
watch riders and horses
at a horse show.
They love horses!

Mandy is a horse rider.
She has a horse
named Jade.
They jump
over a high fence.

Mandy wins the show.
A judge gives her
a trophy and a blue ribbon.
A reporter takes their photo.

Malibu and Brooklyn
meet Mandy and Jade.

"Can you teach us
to be good horse riders?"
Brooklyn asks.
Mandy agrees.

The girls take Jade
to the stables.

Mandy shows them how
to take care of horses.
She grooms Jade.

Malibu learns to
clean a saddle.

Brooklyn learns to
saddle a horse.

The girls try on
special riding clothes.
"You look like
horse riders!"
Mandy says.

They watch a horse
and rider jump
over a fence.

Malibu and Brooklyn
meet Mandy and Jade
back at the stables.

Brooklyn will ride Kiri.

Malibu will ride Misty.

Malibu learns to jump
a high fence with Misty!

Brooklyn and Malibu
will compete in a show!
The girls admire
the awards
Mandy has received.

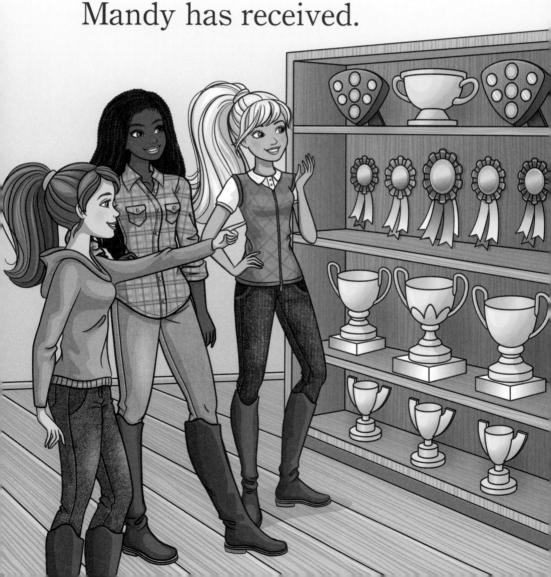

Brooklyn and Malibu
learn that their horses
need days of rest
before the show.

But Malibu and Brooklyn go on a picnic. They take the horses with them.

They ride up a rocky hill.
The girls sit and eat
on a pink blanket.
The horses rest by a tree.

The next day
is the horse show.
The girls are
ready to ride.

But the horses
are unwell.
Mandy calls the vet.

Misty has a hurt hoof
from going up the hill.
The vet wraps it.

Kiri is too tired.
The girls feel bad.

They promise to take
better care of
their horses.

Misty rests for
a few days.

She is all better!
Brooklyn and Mandy
are glad.

Malibu and Brooklyn
keep their promise.

They give their horses
lots of love and care.

Then the girls
and the horses
enter their first show.
They are excited!
Mandy cheers them on.

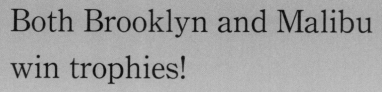

Both Brooklyn and Malibu
win trophies!
"You can be a horse rider!"
says Mandy.